BENNY
AND
PENNY

IN
JUST PRETEND

GEOFFREY HAYES

BENNY
AND
PENNY

IN
JUST PRETEND

A TOON BOOK BY
GEOFFREY HAYES

THE LITTLE LIT LIBRARY, A DIVISION OF RAW JUNIOR, LLC, NEW YORK

For Françoise

Editorial Director: FRANÇOISE MOULY
Advisor: ART SPIEGELMAN

Book Design: FRANÇOISE MOULY & JONATHAN BENNETT

ISBN 13: 978-0-9799238-0-7   ISBN 10: 0-9799238-0-8

10 9 8 7 6 5 4 3 2 1

www.TOON-BOOKS.com

Go away, Penny. I am a pirate!

I can play pirate, too.

10

26

29

And where are
Benny and Penny now?

Here
they
are!

THE END

ABOUT THE AUTHOR

Geoffrey grew up in San Francisco, where he still lives. From an early age, he and his younger brother Rory wrote and illustrated stories for one another.

Geoffrey says, "Like **Benny** I often wanted to play alone. But when I gave in to Rory's demands that I play with him, I was always glad that I did." Both Geoffrey and Rory grew up to be artists.

Geoffrey has written and illustrated over forty children's books, among them the classic *Bear By Himself* and *When the Wind Blew* by Margaret Wise Brown. He is the author of the extremely successful series of early readers *Otto and Uncle Tooth*.